GW00391859

SHERLOCK HOLMES IN GIBRALTAR

The Abandoned Brigantine

and

The Gibraltar Letter

by Sam Benady

GIBRALTAR BOOKS LTD.

GRENDON, NORTHAMPTONSHIRE — GIBRALTAR

First published in Great Britain 1990
by Gibraltar Books Ltd, Rosehill Farm,.
38 Main Road, Grendon, Northants NN7 1JW

British Library Cataloguing in Publication Data
    Benady, Samuel George 1937-
    Sherlock Holmes in Gibraltar
    I. Title
    823.914 [F]

ISBN 0-948466-15-4

Typeset by:- Metropress (Type) Limited, Wellingborough
Printed by:- B.L. & U. Printing, Wellingborough
in association with MN Productions

CONTENTS

EDITOR'S NOTE:

The following documents came into my hands a few years ago, as one of a large bundle of old letters which I purchased, mainly for their philatelic interest, from the estate of an old lady whose grandfather had practised as a physician in Gibraltar. The envelope which contained the document was addressed to the grandfather, and seemed of little interest at the time. It was only recently that I found it in the bottom of a drawer, and on examining it more closely I noticed for the first time a faded inscription in pencil: "From my old friend and fellow student Dr. J. H. Watson M.D." My curiosity aroused, I took out the enclosures and read them. They consisted of the accounts which are printed below. If there was originally a covering letter, it no longer exists.

By one of those coincidences which so often happen in real life, I found an article suggesting a possible cause for the abandonment of the "Mary Celeste" in the British Medical Journal, which arrived on the following day.[1]

A little research confirmed that the old lady's grandfather had indeed studied at Barts, as had Dr. Watson, and that their dates were compatible. Many of the details which are mentioned in the document, such as the marks on the bows of the ship, the sword in the captain's cabin, and Capt. Winchester's experience in Gibraltar appear to be authentic.[2] While this is no proof of the authenticity of the document itself I feel that it deserves publication, if only because it demonstrates how two medical men, although separated by many years in time, can reach such remarkably similar if apparently erroneous conclusions.

The second account is more difficult to verify. The Duke who was abducted must have been the Duke of Connaught, but there is no record of his presence in Gibraltar at the time, nor of his kidnapping. Discretion appears to have been absolute in those days, at least where the Royal family was concerned.

1. J. M. Dunlop. Mary Celeste. *Br Med J* 1987; ii:1036.

2. Report of the Vice-Admiralty Court of Gibraltar. 1872; R. Furneaux. *What Happened on the 'Mary Celeste'*. London: Parrish, 1964.

S. Benady.

THE ABANDONED BRIGANTINE

I

"Yes, Watson," said Mr. Sherlock Holmes, raising his head briefly from his huge book of references, which he had been engaged in cross-indexing. "The sea is indeed mysterious and terrible."

"Most mysterious!" I replied absently, and then started with astonishment as I realised that, yet again, Holmes had penetrated my inmost thoughts.

"Holmes," I expostulated, "How could you possibly have known what was going through my mind? I have said not a word to you for over thirty minutes."

He looked up again with a chuckle. "True, you did not speak," he remarked, "But nevertheless you told me your thoughts as clearly as if you had shouted them from the roof-tops."

"This is too much, Holmes," I exclaimed. "Explain yourself!"

"Only if you promise not to say 'How absurdly simple' when you have heard my explanation."

"Done!"

"When you came into the room," said he, "You were carrying a copy of *The Strand Magazine,* which carries on its cover an illustration of a sailing ship in distress - a brigantine, if I am any judge. You then settled into the armchair and commenced to read. Within minutes, looks of perplexity and then of sadness appeared on your face. You put down the magazine and stared fixedly for a full minute at that picture of a tea clipper which hangs on our wall. You then rose, went to the bookshelf and withdrew one of the volumes which contain the somewhat sensational accounts which you have written of my cases, in particular, the one which includes the cases of the barque *Gloria Scott* and the one which you have chosen to entitle *Black Peter.* Having opened and perused this volume for a while, you returned to your chair, where you sat with an expression of gloom until I ventured to break into your thoughts with my not very profound observation, which merely followed the thoughts which were implicit in your face and actions."

"How absurdly simple —" I began, and then instantly joined him as he laughed heartily.

"Holmes," I said, passing him the magazine, "Have you ever heard of a more mysterious and impenetrable problem than that detailed in these pages?"

He opened the magazine and glanced at the article in question.

"*An Unsolved Mystery.* I see that they have misspelled the name of the ship as usual and no doubt have repeated all the other errors and absurdities which were perpetrated some years ago by some scribbler named Boyle, or Doyle."

"You are acquainted with the case, then?"

"I have some slight recollection of it. Let us look it up in my book of references."

He opened the index volume and scanned it intently.

"Musgrave Ritual," he read. "That was a mysterious and tragic case. Moriarty; plenty of references to him, of course. Mazarin stone, Merton the pugilist — same case, those two. *Matilda Briggs* — another sea story there, Watson. Margolis the strangler. Ah, here it is, *Mary Celeste.*" He selected the appropriate volume, turned over the pages, and handed the heavy volume to me.

I settled down to read the pages which he indicated. They were mainly abstracts of court proceedings and official reports, interspersed with cuttings from newspapers, mainly English and American, but including the *Gibraltar Chronicle* and a few which were presumably from Spanish and Portuguese papers.

"The real facts are certainly more prosaic," I remarked, "But the problem seems no easier to solve."

"Holmes," I continued, as a thought struck me, "Surely you would find it easy to solve the case, which has baffled the whole world for years, by the application of those deductive methods of reasoning which you have so often employed in the past."

"You overestimate my powers, Watson," said Sherlock Holmes, with some amusement, although I could see that he was pleased by the compliment to his abilities. "I do not think that even I could reach the correct solution by pure reasoning from the facts available in these files."

Waving aside my protestations, he lapsed into a thoughtful silence for a few minutes. Then a gleam of amusement appeared in his deep-set eyes.

"Well, Watson," said he, languidly, "Why do you yourself not make an attempt to formulate a hypothesis which will account for the facts? After all, you have been my colleague for many years, ample time to have absorbed the principles of deductive logic of which you speak so highly."

"I certainly shall!" I exclaimed hotly, for I thought I detected some slight irony in his voice. "We shall see whether by tomorrow I cannot present you with a logical explanation for the mysterious happenings on the *Mary Celeste*." With that, I went to my room, taking the book of references with me.

"We shall see." said Sherlock Holmes thoughtfully, as I left.

II

On the following morning I rose late, after a largely sleepless night. A wintry December sun shone through the windows of our rooms in Baker Street. Holmes was already at the breakfast table. He looked up as I entered.

"A fine day, Watson," said he cheerfully, "Have you made any progress with the intellectual problem you have set yourself?"

"Indeed I have," I rejoined, somewhat coolly, "And I will give you a full account of my solution as soon as I have had some breakfast."

A little later, when we were seated in our armchairs, Holmes looked at me expectantly.

I arranged my papers in front of me. "The first thing to do," I said, I dare say somewhat self-importantly, "Is to marshal the relevant facts.

The *Mary Celeste* left New York on November the 7th '72 with a cargo of methylated spirits for Genoa. Her captain was Benjamin S. Briggs, who was accompanied by his wife and child. There was a crew of eight men. She was sighted by the brigantine *Dei Gratia* on December the 5th, derelict and abandoned, some 400 miles east of the Azores, and was boarded and taken into Gibraltar by a prize-crew from the latter vessel. At the subsequent hearing by the Vice-Admiralty Court in Gibraltar, it was established that the ship was sea-worthy, although she bore every sign of having been hastily abandoned. There was no sign of violence on board."

Holmes stirred in his seat. "Was there not a sword found in the captain's cabin?" he asked.

"There was, but it was in its scabbard, and stains found on it were analysed and found not to be blood. It was an Italian sword, with a cross of Savoy on the hilt, and was thought to be a souvenir acquired by Captain Briggs on his travels."

"Pray continue with your exposition."

"The last entry on the log slate was for 25th November, giving the ship's position as six miles to the north of Santa Maria island in the Azores. The ship's boat was missing, and all the signs were that the ship had been abandoned hurriedly. There was no indication why this might have been done, and no trace of the boat or the crew has ever been found."

"I seem to recall that there were some strange marks on the hull."

"I cannot explain those," I admitted, "Each side of the bows had an almost symmetrical strip shaved off just above the water-line. I suppose that this could have been caused by rocks, during a near-ship-wreck in the Azores, but all accounts state that the strips appeared very regular, as if they had been cut by a sharp instrument."

"What then is your solution to the mystery?"

I leaned backwards in my armchair. "I think that we can discard theories involving the slaughter of the crew by pirates, for the Atlantic has been free of these for almost a century. Mutiny by the ship's crew, or their murder by the crew of the *Dei Gratia* for the salvage money, which was the theory put forward by the Admiralty Advocate in Gibraltar, seems even more unlikely; in all these cases, signs of a struggle would surely have been found. I am prepared to discount theories of sea-monsters rising from the deep to swallow up the crew —"

"Are you?" said Sherlock Holmes, and smiled.

A little nettled, I continued, "The only remaining possibility, then, seems to be that the ship was abandoned voluntarily because of some danger to those on board her, and that the ship's boat was then swamped and all on board drowned. But the *Mary Celeste* was seaworthy when found, although there had been a storm and the rigging and sails were damaged. I do not believe that an experienced captain, as all agree Captain Briggs was, would put those in his charge to the perils of an Atlantic storm in a small boat unless his ship were actually foundering, or if those on board were in deadly danger."

"You appear to have eliminated your last possibility," Holmes observed.

"Not quite," I replied triumphantly, "The sea is not the only possible source of peril to those on board a ship. A situation may have arisen on board which seemed so dangerous to the captain that he saw no alternative but to risk his wife and child, and his crew, to the fury of the Atlantic waves. Indeed, it has been suggested, on the strength of some minor damage to one of the casks in the cargo, that an explosion of spirit fumes may have been feared, and that the captain may have decided to launch the ship's boat and stand off from the ship until the fumes had dissipated, and that the *Mary Celeste* then drifted away, leaving them to their fate."

"But this, I take it, is not your preferred solution." Holmes observed.

"Indeed not," said I, "The evidence for a serious leak of methylated spirit is very poor, and in any case, I cannot imagine that seasoned seamen such as Captain Briggs and his crew would not have taken the precaution of fastening a tow-line to the ship. It is true that a tow-line might have snapped, but no trace of this was found aboard the ship.

"The true solution to the mystery was suggested to me by a remark which you once made during the case of the missing racehorse Silver Blaze, to the effect that sometimes it is not the presence but the absence of something which may be significant."

Holmes clapped his hands in approval.

"Excellent, Watson, excellent!" he cried. "I see that you have taken note of my methods, even while you were recounting them to the public in so sensational a manner. I believe there is hope for you yet."

Thus encouraged, I continued, "Those who boarded the abandoned vessel described in great detail what they found on her, but nowhere is there any mention of an animal on board. Now, there can be very few vessels which do not carry one or more cats on board, to keep down the rats, and frequently also a dog, to guard the ship against intruders when it is in port —"

"Might these animals not have been taken into the boat by the crew?"

"The *Mary Celeste* was abandoned in such haste that all personal belongings were left behind. There was then surely no time to hunt down the ship's pets. No, Holmes, the explanation for the absence of the animals is more sinister: I believe that these creatures had become infected with rabies, or hydrophobia, and this so terrorised the crew that in a mad panic they took to the boat, which was then swamped with the loss of all aboard. As the disease progressed, the rabid animals then jumped or fell overboard, leaving the ship deserted and a mystery which has remained unsolved — until today!" I added with some satisfaction.

"Capital, Watson, capital!" exclaimed Sherlock Holmes with a broad smile, "You have excelled yourself!"

"Do you then agree with me that I have divined the solution to this hitherto insoluble problem?" I inquired.

"Indeed not! But your solution is ingenious, and not entirely devoid of logical reasoning."

Somewhat crestfallen, I persisted.

"How can you maintain, then, that mine is not a possible solution?"

"For at least four reasons."

"Four!" I exclaimed, wounded. "Come, Holmes, I cannot believe that you have found so many flaws in my theory. Let us hear them!"

"Very well," said Holmes languidly. "*Primus.* I cannot believe that a crew of able-bodied men, used to facing all the dangers of the sea, would flee in panic from rabid animals into the greater danger of an Atlantic storm, rather than banding together with knives, boathooks and belaying-pins to hunt the creatures down. *Secundus.* Should they indeed have decided to flee, which would presuppose not only cowardice but stupidity, as they would have been exposed to attack by the creatures while they laboured to launch the ship's boat, they would surely have seized every weapon available in order to defend themselves. Yet the sword remained in the cabin. *Tertius.* I think we must assume that there were several animals, even to attempt to justify this improbable panic. Yet the *Mary Celeste* was not found to be in total disorder, as it would have been had these creatures run wild through it in their final frenzy, prior to casting themselves so conveniently overboard."

He paused for a second, and I returned to the attack.

"Your fourth reason, Holmes. Which is your fourth reason? Your first three only make my solution improbable, not impossible."

"My fourth reason you may well find more convincing. I *know* that matters did not proceed as you have conjectured, for I was on board the *Mary Celeste* on that fateful voyage."

I stared at Sherlock Holmes in disbelief.

"Holmes, that is impossible!" I ejaculated. "You were surely too young —"

"I was young," he agreed, "But not too young. I will recount to you what truly happened, but only on the condition that it remain a secret during the lifetime of all those involved."

"You may rely on me." said I earnestly.

13

III

The Lily of Aosta

Holmes rose, and filled his pipe from the Persian slipper on the mantelpiece. When he had returned to his seat, he lit the pipe, and spent some minutes smoking it thoughtfully. I was in a fever of impatience to hear his tale, but I knew better than to interrupt his reverie.

Finally he broke the silence.

"I have rarely spoken to you about my early life, Watson," said he, "And it is possible that you do not know that, after my schooling was completed, I spent a year abroad before going up to Cambridge. I had already determined to devote my life to the study of criminology, and considered that I might benefit from a period of apprenticeship in an organisation recognised as the foremost detective agency in the world."

"You mean —"

"Exactly, Watson, the Pinkerton Detective Agency. I must confess, though, that I was seriously disappointed; our American cousins show a sad deficiency of imagination both as criminals and as detectives. But I run ahead of my story.

* * *

My brother Mycroft, who even then had connections the world over, was instrumental in securing for me a junior position in the agency, and I sailed for New York early in '72.

A few months at the agency convinced me that I had nothing to learn from them about scientific detection, and I would have left and returned to England had I not been so fascinated by the energy and zest for life of the citizens of New York. Nevertheless, I was approaching a state of total *ennui* when one morning, a young man of swarthy complexion strode into the office.

He stopped at the doorway, and stared at me in amazement.

'Sherlock,' he cried 'Can it possibly be you?'

For a second I had not recognised him, for since I had last seen him he had acquired a bristling black moustache. It was Luca D'Este, a young Italian of noble blood who had been a companion of my schooldays.

'Luca,' I exclaimed, grasping him warmly by the hand, 'What can have brought you here, so far from the Mediterranean sun which you always swore to return to and never leave again?

'It is a matter of honour — my family's honour, and a lady's honour, he replied seriously, 'May I speak with you privately; I remember your keen mind and your energy of old, and I feel sure that you are the only man who can help me in this strange quest.'

I led him into an inner office, where, throwing himself into a chair, he launched himself impatiently into his tale.

'You may know, Sherlock, that I am a close relative of the King of Italy. Two years ago, his son, Amadeo of Savoy, Duke of Aosta, was chosen by the Spanish Parliament to be King of Spain. I travelled to that country with my cousin, as part of his entourage. Also in his party, as one of the ladies-in-waiting to his Queen, Maria Victoria, was a young girl of sixteen, who even at that early age, because of her surpassing beauty, was known as the Lily of Aosta; her name is Bianca Bernini.

'If you have followed the fortunes of Spain in the last year, you will know that the King's reign has not been easy; ignored and insulted by Madrid society, his rule threatened by Carlists and Republicans, he has become discouraged, and abandoning his high hopes of improving and modernising Spain through a popular constitutional monarchy, has retreated more and more into the company of those Italians who form his court. His eye lighted on Bianca; he became infatuated with her, until terrified by his advances the girl, virtuous and loyal to her queen, fled from the palace. Would that she had confided in me,' Luca groaned, 'She has not been seen since.'

'How then do you know of all this?' I asked.

'As soon as her disappearance was known, the King summoned me and confided to me what had happened. We had high words —'

'You are then very fond of the lady.' I observed.

His dark eyes flashed in astonishment.

'How did you know?' said he.

'One does not exchange angry words with a king, even if he is a cousin, for any lesser reason.' I observed drily. 'Proceed.'

'He begged me, for the honour of the family, and because of a very natural concern about Bianca, for he feels the deepest remorse about his behaviour to her, to spare no effort to find her and bring her to safety.'

'And how did this quest bring you to New York?'

'I soon found out, for Madrid is a hotbed of spies and gossip-mongers, that Bianca had been abducted by a group of Republicans. Their plan is either to hold her to ransom, or to force her to make public the conduct of the King, to further discredit him and the monarchy in the eyes of the Spaniards. Fearing that I was on their trail, they spirited her away to Vigo, and thence to New York, where a group of Republican *emigrés* have established themselves. I followed, hot on their heels, and have discovered that she is being held, under close guard, in an apartment not far from here.'

'Why then, you have done all the detection yourself,' said I, 'All we need to do is to call on the excellent New York Police Department and they will release your beloved.'

'That is impossible,' said Luca, 'Firstly, Bianca's life must not be put at risk; these men are desperate, and might well murder her if they feared capture —'

'And secondly, if the story of her capture and release were to reach the ears of the pertinacious American press, your cousin the King might be embarrassed, so you thought that it would be best to trust to the discretion of a private enquiry agency.' I interposed. 'Very well then, we must resort to subterfuge.'

'You will then help me yourself? It would be more discreet if we were able to keep even this agency out of it.'

'Of course.'

Luca told me that he had observed the house in which Bianca was imprisoned. The apartment was on the second floor, and at all times there were at least three men guarding it. He had seen them going in and out, and it was only with difficulty, because of his concern for the lady's safety, that he had restrained himself from rushing in and confronting the ruffians on his own

My plan was simple. On that very night we made our way to the building, and having introduced ourselves surreptitiously, with the aid of a jemmy, into the hall, crept up the stairs until we were outside the door of the apartment. A murmur of voices could be heard inside.

I knelt down, and placing an armful of rags and papers, which I had brought with me, by the door, set a light to them. Waiting only until I could see the smoke beginning to seep under the door, I put on my best Yankee accent, and on a hysterical note, shouted: 'Fire! The building's alight! Fire!'

There was a confused babble of voices inside. Luca and I stationed ourselves on each side of the door, clutching heavy cudgels. The door burst open and three men rushed out. Luca's cudgel came down on the head of the first, and he collapsed to the floor without a sound. The other two were burdened with a form wrapped in a blanket, which could only be the drugged body of the girl; before they could put her down and defend themselves, we were on them, and they too fell senseless. Pausing only to verify that it was indeed Bianca, and that she breathed, we carried her out of the house and into a waiting cab, and drove away from the scene.

Our next problem was to get Bianca and Luca back to Europe without attracting the attention of her abductors, or the Press. Luca agreed that it would be best to return to Italy, and restore Bianca to her family; a return to Spain would only expose her to further danger. I therefore left my friend, with the aid of my Irish landlady, to look after the rapidly recovering Bianca in my room, and made my way to the waterfront early in the morning. There I ascertained that a cargo ship, the brigantine *Mary Celeste*, was leaving for Genoa two days later. The steam-packet to Lisbon, which was leaving on that very day, I rejected, as I did not wish for Bianca to return to the Iberian peninsula, and it seemed to me that the gang would assume that we would attempt to escape from New York by this means, and would be prepared to intercept us, but I boarded her and handed the captain a package, with instructions to forward it urgently on arrival in Lisbon.

I then sought out the captain of the *Mary Celeste*. I found Captain Briggs in a nearby lodging house with his wife and child. Captain Winchester, who was a part owner of the ship, was with them. Enjoining all to the utmost secrecy, I explained only that a lady and a gentleman, who were being pursued by criminals, desired immediate passage to Europe, for which they would pay a generous fee.

'Oh, Ben,' cried Mrs. Briggs to her husband, 'We must help this unfortunate young couple. I would never forgive myself if they came to any harm because of our failure to assist them.'

Her husband and his partner, who had seemed about to demur, were swayed by her appeal, and the transaction was agreed.

'Say,' added Mrs. Briggs, 'Why don't your friends come and join us here? They'll be safer in company than alone.'

I doubted this, as Bianca's pursuers would surely be haunting the area of the waterfront to foil any attempt at escape. We finally agreed that I would bring the passengers to the lodging house after dark on the following night, so that they might board the ship just before she sailed on the morning tide.

At Briggs' invitation, I accompanied him to the ship, where I met the crew, assuring myself that all were genuine seamen, and well-known to their captain. In particular the mate Richardson seemed a fine example of an honest, fearless Yankee mariner.

Returning to my apartment, I found Bianca fully recovered from her ordeal. As she attempted to thank me in pretty, broken English, I was able to observe her properly for the first time. She had the flaw-less, creamy skin and clear grey eyes which can often be observed in northern Italy, but combined with such perfect features as I have never seen before or since. Long, silky black hair, and a lissome figure, just above the medium height, completed the picture. As she became con-scious of my gaze, she lowered her eyes, and the colour which flooded her cheeks seemed to add a further dimension to her beauty.

With Luca's assistance, she described to me how she had been way-laid as she rushed out of the palace, and confined in the cellar of a house in Madrid, from which she was taken to Vigo, where she and her captors embarked for New York. They had not used her ill, as they hoped to force her to make public a statement discrediting the King. This the brave girl had refused to do, but the constant brow-beating which she received because of this, together with her prolonged incar-ceration and the frequent soporifics administered in order to prevent her calling for help, had no doubt accentuated the natural pallor of her features.

After dark on the following evening a cab took us to Captain Briggs' lodging. As we approached, I noticed three sinister figures lurking on the other side of the road. It was clear that the house was being watched, and that my plan must be changed. As the cab halted, I quickly told the driver to drive to the rear of the building after we had alighted. We entered the lodging house, and I paused to warn Briggs of the watchers outside.

'I reckon I can take care of myself.' said he with a laugh.

There was no time for argument; we ran swiftly to the back of the house, and jumped into the cab, which was waiting outside the back door, which fortunately did not appear to be watched. I ordered the cab-driver to take us to the *Mary Celeste*, and we boarded the ship. The mate, although surprised to see us, made us welcome, and installed Bianca in the captain's cabin, which it had been agreed she should share with Mrs. Briggs and the child.

I explained to Richardson what had happened, and that I feared that the captain and his family might be at grave risk from our pursuers.

'Let us go to his lodging and deal with the ruffians outside,' said he. 'I will give instructions to the men to guard the ship, and the lady. Then we will be off.'

Luca remained, with drawn sword, outside the cabin door, and Richardson and I made our way swiftly to the lodging house. There was no sign of the watchers.

With grim foreboding we entered the house. The door of the room

19

occupied by the captain and his family was ajar. As we entered the room a dreadful sight met our eyes. By the light of a fire which was even then spreading to the curtains we could see that Briggs and his wife had been savagely stabbed to death as they slept. As we recoiled in horror, the dry wood of the timber wall caught fire and the room became a sheet of flame. We turned to flee, and then the mate caught sight of the child, peacefully asleep in a cot by her murdered parents' bed.

'Sophia!' he cried, leaping forward through the flames, and snatching the child from the cot, he followed me out of the burning house.

As we gained the roadway, the whole building became enveloped in flames. None of the other occupants can have had any chance of survival.

Soberly, we returned to the ship. Although we kept a keen lookout, we could detect no signs of pursuit, and it seemed likely to me that the murderers could have been deceived in the darkness, thinking that they had killed Bianca and Luca in the house, or that they had perished in the conflagration intended to hide the crime.

Once aboard, we held a council of war. Bianca took the bewildered and weeping child into her arms and attempted to console her. Richardson, once we had told him the whole story, suggested that we should proceed with the voyage as planned, and I was inclined to agree, as any attempt to report the murders and arson would inevitably cause us to be detained indefinitely in New York, and would undoubtedly expose Bianca and Luca to the publicity which they were so desperate to avoid.

'But what shall we do with the child?' asked Luca.

Bianca looked up with flashing eyes.

'Because of me her parents die,' she said fervently, 'I will take her and give her a new life!'

'We both will,' said Luca, and took her hand.

She lifted her eyes to him with a brilliant smile which said more than words could."

* * *

IV

Sherlock Holmes paused at this point, and puffed reflectively at his pipe.

'If I might make a deduction of my own at this point, Holmes,' I said, somewhat mischievously, 'Your description of the girl, Bianca, seems to indicate that you were considerably attracted to her.'

'You must remember that I was very young,' said Holmes tartly, 'In any case the difference between us — '

'You mean because she was of the nobility — '

'No, Watson, because she was by far my intellectual inferior. But let me proceed with my story.

* * *

The *Mary Celeste* sailed with the morning tide. The next two weeks were uneventful, if any crossing of the Atlantic by sailing ship in winter can be said to be uneventful. Bianca and the child Sophia became great friends, and the ship frequently rang with their merry laughter. There was no sign of pursuit, yet I was not entirely at ease. It seemed likely that our pursuers would not long be deceived, and would find some way to follow us, and I spent many long hours on deck scanning the horizon through a telescope.

As it happened, however, it was not I who made the first sighting. As we approached the island of Santa Maria, which is the southernmost of the Azores, there was a cry from the other side of the deck. It was Bianca.

'A monster! A monster rises from the sea!'

I ran to her side. A great grey mass was emerging from the waves — your hypothetical monster, Watson. It was only a few yards away, and I could see that it was no sea-monster, but a man-made construction. Without doubt it was a submarine vessel, such as are now being constructed by all the great navies in the world, but at that time it was, as far as I knew, merely an inventor's pipe-dream. Was it friend or foe? We were not left long in doubt.

With a clanking sound, a hatch on the upper surface of the vessel opened, and a bearded face peered forth.

'Ees the brigantina *Mary Celeste*? Señor Holmes accompanied by two friends of the King of Espain?' it enquired cautiously.

'Who are you?' I called out.

'I am Don Narciso Monturiol, and this is my invento the submarino, the *Ictíneo III*. I have been charged by the King to escort you to where you wish to go.'

'How did you know that we were on this ship?' I persisted, still a little suspicious.

'The King has received a message from you, from Lisboa.'

I breathed a sigh of relief. My message had arrived safely.

'We welcome your escort, Don Narciso,' I cried.

Monturiol and I agreed that my companions and I should remain on board the *Mary Celeste*, as the submarine would be rather uncomfortable, especially for a young lady and a child. He would patrol in our vicinity and report to us if he detected any vessel following us.

A few days after we had left the Azores behind, the submarine again surfaced near us. By this time, the weather had worsened considerably, with high seas and poor visibility, but Monturiol was able to make us understand that there was a brigantine following closely on our course, and that he proposed to take Bianca and Luca aboard.

'If the ship indeed carries our pursuers,' said Luca, 'Then anyone left aboard the *Mary Celeste* is doomed, for in their fury that we have escaped them they will surely kill all those who have assisted us.'

'You are right,' said Richardson, 'Can we not all be carried by the underwater vessel? We could then leave them to chase an empty ship, giving us more time to make our escape.'

Monturiol confirmed that there was sufficient room in the submarine for us and the crew, and proceeded to attempt to bring his vessel alongside our ship. Because of the gale and the high seas, this proved extremely difficult. Twice the submarine came alongside, and on both occasions was flung violently against the bows, gouging deep strips out of the timber with its steel fins.

Finally, seeing that any further attempt was likely to endanger the submarine, Richardson shouted to the vessel to stand off: we would lower the ship's boat and row across to it.

This was done with great difficulty. More than once the boat was almost swamped by the waves, but eventually we reached the submarine. First the child and then Bianca were pulled through the hatch into safety; then Luca clambered in. As he turned to give me his hand in assistance, a tremendous wave hit the submarine, driving it into the boat, which was crushed, and all those in it were engulfed by the waves. I received a blow on the head, and was barely conscious of all this, and only afterwards was I told how Luca had kept his grip on my arm through it all and had dragged me to safety. We circled the area for some time, but no trace of the crew did we find. My good friend Richardson and his men had given their lives for us. Then the shape of the pursuing brigantine began to loom up through the mist, and Monturiol gave the order to dive.

'What was the name of the ship which you sighted?' I asked the inventor.

'The *Dei Gratia*.' said he.

As our journey proceeded, I questioned Monturiol about his marvellous vessel, and found him most willing to expound on his invention.

'For more than one decade I have worked,' he said, 'And I started with a small wooden vessel driven by pedals; after, I build a big one, with steam engine, but that one also could only work in calm water, in harbour, and the Ministry of Marine are not interested. So I have worked for years on this third *submarino*, which will travel under the ocean.'

'And very successful you have been!' I exclaimed.

'Alas no,' said the inventor sadly, '*Ictíneo* is leaking badly after the heavy seas and the collision with your ship; she is taking in much water, and will be hard-pressed to bring us to the Espanish coast. Fear not,' he added, 'We shall be safe. But *Ictíneo* will never sail again, and the Navy will again pour scorn on my efforts. This will be my last *submarino*.'

'Never fear,' I rejoined. 'If not you, someone else will take up your work, and perfect it.'

* * *

'And I was right, Watson.' added Sherlock Holmes.

* * *

A few years later, one Isaac Peral, a compatriot of Monturiol's, built an improved submarine, and since then many other countries have followed suit, and the submarine is now an important part of the world's navies.

Monturiol was true to his word, and landed us all safely and secretly at a small port near Cadiz, from where, with the help of letters which he carried from the King, Monturiol was able to arrange for a fast frigate of the Spanish Navy to take Bianca and Luca to Genoa, while I hastened to Madrid to report to King Amadeo.

'I am deeply grateful to you, Mr. Holmes,' said Amadeo, 'And I am happy that the wrong which I did has been righted. It is only just that I should have gained no benefit from all this. In a month or two I shall abdicate and return to Italy. From what you tell me, it seems that I may well be able to attend my cousin's wedding!'

While in Madrid I heard that the *Mary Celeste* had been taken into Gibraltar by the crew of the *Dei Gratia*, who had obviously decided to try to make a profit out of the affair. More disquieting news was that Captain Winchester had been called to Gibraltar to testify. I felt sure that he intended to keep his promise to say nothing of our transaction, but feared that the lawyers might wheedle out of him more than he intended to say. I travelled south again, to Gibraltar, and attended the court in disguise. Afterwards, I revealed myself to Winchester and learned from him that the deaths of Captain and Mrs. Briggs had passed unnoticed, as he alone knew that they had been staying in the ill-fated hotel, and it was assumed in New York that they had sailed on the *Mary Celeste*. Although he assured me that he would stand firm and say nothing, I thought it best to suggest to him that the court intended to arrest him for complicity in the murder of the crew of the *Mary Celeste*. He took fright and fled to America, taking no further part in the case.

The *Dei Gratia* sailed on to Genoa, even while the Admiralty Court was hearing the case, and much to the annoyance of the Judge Advocate. The Republican ruffians, knowing the proposed destination of the *Mary Celeste*, presumably suspected that Bianca and Luca, if they had survived, would make their way to that port, and were determined to have their revenge on them. Their deductions were correct as it happened, but the delay in Gibraltar meant that Luca and the Genoese *carabinieri* were waiting for them when they arrived, and the scoundrels paid the ultimate penalty for their crimes. The ship and its corrupt crew returned to Gibraltar, where the court obviously had serious doubts as to the *bona fides* of the salvagers, but nothing could be proved, and the Judge had to be satisfied with granting only a minuscule salvage award.

'Ah, yes, Watson, one other point. There *was* a ship's cat. It too found its way to safety - in the arms of Miss Sophia Briggs who, by the way, was adopted by Bianca and Luca D'Este after their marriage. She is now the Duchess of ——.'

* * *

25

THE GIBRALTAR LETTER

Many of the accounts which I have written about the exploits of my good friend Mr. Sherlock Holmes were never intended for publication, especially those involving matters of state and those whose publication might cause suffering to innocent parties. I have been careful to record all such cases, however, and have deposited them in my dispatch box in the vaults of Cox's Bank in Charing Cross. One day, perhaps, when it is safe to do so, these accounts may be collated and published by some future historian of scientific detection.

I first heard the story of the affair of the Gibraltar letter from Holmes some years after it happened. We had been sitting in our chambers in Baker Street one cold winter's evening, pleasantly relaxed after one of Mrs. Hudson's substantial and delicious meals, when I rose reluctantly and went to the mantelpiece to retrieve my pipe.

"Be a good fellow and toss me my tobacco, Watson," said Sherlock Holmes languidly, stretching out an arm.

I reached for the Persian slipper where Holmes habitually kept his shag, and grasped it by the tip. To my surprise, I felt a hard irregular object wedged in the pointed toe.

"Why, there's something here that certainly is not tobacco!" I said, as I probed with my forefinger into the depths of the slipper. Holmes watched with some amusement as I withdrew the mysterious object on the tip of my finger. It was a gold ring, set with a magnificent ruby.

"Really, Holmes," I cried, "I thought that I had become inured to your Bohemian habits, but to use a valuable object like this so carelessly -"

"Ah, but my use of this ring was quite logical," replied my friend with a smile, "It was the only object which I could find which would fit snugly into the toe of the slipper."

"But why -?"

"Because there is a hole in the slipper, through which most of my tobacco is at this moment falling on to the carpet," said Holmes tartly.

A little chagrined, I bent over to pick up the scattered tobacco, remarking, I dare say somewhat peevishly, "A valuable ring like this one should be better guarded."

"On the contrary, it was very safely kept there," replied Holmes. "It has been there since we first met, and you have never noticed it before."

"But how did it come into your possession? A family heirloom, perhaps," I hazarded.

"Indeed not. It was a gift from an august personage, in gratitude for a service which I was able to perform." He gazed at the ceiling and puffed reflectively at his pipe. I waited patiently and after a while he began to recount the story which I have recorded here.

* * *

It happened in '76 — some years before your time, Watson. One day I received a note from my brother Mycroft, summoning me to his club. You know the Diogenes Club, that haven for the unsociable, where no talking is permitted save in the Strangers' Room. Mycroft met me there, and motioned me to an armchair.

'You have been to Gibraltar before,' he began, eyeing me keenly.

'Only very briefly, during the affair of the *Mary Celeste*,' I replied. 'But from your choice of words, I deduce that you wish me to go again.'

'Not I, Sherlock, but I have a most urgent request, I might almost say a command, from a certain gracious lady -'

'You need say no more,' I interrupted. 'Tell me what I must do.'

'Since your knowledge of history, except the history of criminal activity, is sketchy to say the least, you may not be aware that the fortress of Gibraltar was captured from Spain in 1704, and ceded to the British Crown by the Treaty of Utrecht in 1713. Since then Spain has attempted on many occasions to regain the Rock, but has always been foiled by British diplomacy or British valour, and each successive defence of Gibraltar has brought it closer to the heart of the average Englishman, so that now any British Government which proposed to return the place to Spain would be faced with such a public outcry that it would be forced to resign in short order.

'In the early days, however, Parliament had less power, and the Crown had correspondingly more. George I was under constant pressure from his Spanish counterpart Philip V to return Gibraltar to Spain, and indeed some of his own Ministers held that this, in exchange for a treaty, would be to Britain's advantage. In response to these pressures, King George publicly wrote letters to Philip promising to cede back the fortress, but only if the British Parliament should give its approval, which he knew it was most unlikely to do. This did not satisfy the Spanish king, who continued to press with the obstinacy of a weak and ailing man, and in the end our King wrote a secret letter promising that the British Crown would consent to return the Rock to Spain after 150 years, provided only that Spain pressed its claim by presenting this letter within a year of the expiry of this period.

'The letter was never delivered to Philip, although rumours of it must have reached the Spanish Court. Before it could be sent, he lost patience with diplomacy and besieged Gibraltar. Instead George sent the letter to the Governor of Gibraltar, the Earl of Portmore, possibly thinking that it might prove to be a useful bargaining counter if the siege went badly for the defenders.

'In the event, the Spanish attack failed, but in the chaos of the siege the letter was misplaced and never found. Thought to have been accidentally destroyed, it was almost forgotten and in the aftermath of defeat Philip never dared to renew his demand, and George was no doubt only too glad to forget its existence.'

'I take it that the letter has reappeared,' I remarked.

'Of course!' snapped Mycroft. 'I would hardly have mentioned it otherwise. The problem is that it has disappeared again, and so has its finder. And he is a Royal Duke — the Duke of C —!' he added with a groan.

So it was that less than a week later I found myself stepping ashore at Gibraltar on a bright autumn morning from one of Her Majesty's fastest frigates. I was met on the quayside by the Governor's son and aide-de-camp, Robert Napier. He lost no time in explaining what had happened, during the short carriage ride to the Governor's residence, known as the Convent, and while we waited for His Excellency the Governor, Lord Napier of Magdala.

'The Duke arrived in Gibraltar in October '75, just over a year ago, and left in the spring of this year with his brother, the Prince of Wales, who was on his way back to England after touring India. A few weeks ago he suddenly returned to Gibraltar unannounced and in secret. Of course my father invited him to stay in the Convent. One evening shortly after his arrival, he retired to his room early, taking down a book of seventeenth century sermons from the book-case in his room to read in bed. Hidden between the pages of this book he found a letter. Quickly realising what it was that he had found, he took it down to the Governor, and read it aloud to us.'

'Who was present when it was read out?' I enquired.

'His Excellency, myself and my mother only.'

'No one else at all?' I persisted.

'Oh, there were servants in and out of the room at the time, who might have heard part of it -"

'Who were these servants?'

'Absolutely trustworthy, Mr. Holmes. You need not seek a traitor among them. Only my father's batman, Barker, who has been with him for many years, and a Gibraltarian maid, Conchita Demaya, who has served the Convent faithfully since she was a girl, could possibly have heard anything.'

'Very well. What happened next?'

'Before he finished, the Duke appeared to realise how dangerous the document might be. He stopped reading, folded it and placed it in his pocket, saying that he would take it to England on his return, for it was of great historical interest, but that it should be kept safe until then.'

'And is it in fact such a dangerous document?' I asked.

'Indeed it is, Mr. Holmes,' boomed a new voice, as the imposing figure of Lord Napier of Magdala walked into the room. 'The letter gave an unequivocal promise from the Crown of Great Britain that the sovereignty of Gibraltar would be transferred to Spain on its presentation before the end of the year 1876 — this year, Mr. Holmes! Her Majesty would feel morally obliged to honour this undertaking by her ancestor, and this would inevitably bring her into constitutional conflict with her Ministers. Even if the Prime Minister bowed to her wishes, the public anger which the cession of the Rock would arouse would surely cause the fall of the Government and further decrease the Crown's popularity, which is already at a low ebb. And now the Duke has disappeared — and the letter has gone with him!'

'Ah, yes, the disappearance of the Duke. Tell me how this happened, your Excellency,' I said.

'That evening, the Duke returned to his room, taking the letter with him. On the following day he rode to the Cork Woods in Spain with a groom -' Lord Napier hesitated, looking decidedly uncomfortable.

'Come, my lord! I must have all the information in this case, however embarrassing it may be,' said I firmly.

The Governor's already high colour deepened to purple, and he seemed ready to explode with rage at my temerity. Then he passed his hand over his brow and sat down. When he spoke, he had regained control of himself:

'You are young, Mr. Holmes, and you come highly recommended, so I will try to make allowances for your manner. You are right, of course. You must have all the facts at your disposal, even though what I am about to tell you I have not even dared to report to Her Majesty.' Lord Napier hesitated still, and I said helpfully:

'You are about to tell me that the Duke left a mistress here, or in Spain, whom he could not forget when he returned to England, hence his unexpected return.'

'Robert! You did not -'

Lord Napier's son quickly shook his head.

'It was merely a logical deduction, Lord Napier,' said I reassuring-ly. 'What other information would you feel justified in concealing from your Monarch? But pray continue with your story. I presume that you do not believe that the Duke has simply eloped with this person.'

'No, that is inconceivable. The Duke's sense of duty would forbid it, although I believe that he is very deeply enamoured of the lady, who is a young and beautiful widow named Ana Pedroz. During his previous stay in Gibraltar, he used to visit her regularly after riding with the Royal Calpe Hunt. On this occasion, he rode with his usual groom, Pepe Ansaldo, a Gibraltarian, to the village of Gaucín where this lady lives, in the hills above the Cork Woods, and dined at the 'Hostal Inglés' which is a hostelry popular with the officers of the garrison. There the groom remained with the owner, one Pedro Real, who is his distant relative, while the Duke visited Señora Pedroz.

'When he did not return on the following morning as arranged, Ansaldo was alarmed and went to the house of the Duke's lover which stands on its own some distance away from the village. There was nobody there, and the house had obviously been ransacked. Do you think that the abductors, whoever they are, could have found the let-ter? We searched for it high and low in the Duke's bedroom here, and in Señora Pedroz' house, but it was not to be found.'

'I think we can assume that the abductors made their attack because they knew of the letter; for mere thieves or *bandoleros* would not have abducted the Duke without demanding a ransom. If this is so, it is quite evident that it cannot have been found, else it would not have been necessary to abduct the Duke and the woman,' I replied. 'They were certainly alive when they were removed, for there would have been no reason to carry away dead bodies, although of course they may not be by now.'

'Surely no Spaniard would dare to assassinate an English Royal Duke!' Robert Napier burst out, his voice full of horror.

'We must consider every possibility,' I said gravely. 'If the letter and the abduction are connected, and we must assume that they are, who would be most interested in getting their hands on this letter?'

'Every Spaniard dreams of regaining Gibraltar for his country,' said Lord Napier heavily, 'And there are many political groups which would see the advantage of having the credit for such an achievement. The young King Alfonso XII is an honourable man, who would probably much prefer not to use a document obtained in such a dastardly way, but if it were offered to him publicly he would be forced to act on it lest the recently restored Bourbon dynasty of Spain be again swept away by popular discontent.'

'For the agreement offered in the letter to be valid, it must be presented before the end of this year, that is to say in less than two months,' said I, 'This makes the matter most urgent, for every day that these villains do not have the letter in their hands will make them more Impatient, and this may drive them to desperate acts. I must start the investigation immediately.'

I was shown to the bedroom used by the Duke. As Lord Napier said, it had been thoroughly searched: even the panelling had been removed from the wall. I asked for the book where the letter had been found. It was a volume of Donne's sermons, and it fell open easily at a page which was stained by the imprint of a document which had lain there for many years. Obviously the book had not been read for a century and a half, or the letter would have come to light earlier.

'Are you not wasting your time here?' asked Robert Napier curiously. 'Nothing can remain undiscovered in this room. surely. Should we not go to Gaucín and seek traces of the Duke there? He must have carried the letter with him, for he obviously realised its importance. Perhaps he hid it somewhere in the hostelry where he dined, or in his mistress'- in Ana Pedroz' house.'

'All in good time. Tell me, did the Duke keep a diary?'

'Yes, it is here where we found it, on his bedside table. We examined it closely but there were no recent entries.'

I examined the journal. The last entry was dated several days before the Duke's disappearance. A torn edge showed that the next page had been ripped.

'Look at this!' I said.

'We noticed that, of course,' said Napier a little impatiently. 'The page was nowhere to be found. We will never know what was written there, if indeed anything was.'

'Ah, but you are wrong,' said I triumphantly, holding the diary up at an angle to the midday sun, which was streaming in from the window. 'See, when the Duke wrote he bore down heavily with his pen at times, and this has left an impression on the following page.'

Napier's eyes lit up, and he came up to my shoulder as we struggled to make out the words impressed on the blank page.

'...Cannot bear to destroy...enormous historical importance... dangerous in wrong hands...must hide it safely...' we read with great difficulty. Then the faint marks became illegible except for one word 'friend'.

'My word. but you have a keen eye, Mr. Holmes' He must have destroyed the page on which he wrote in order to leave no clue to the hiding place he chose,' cried Robert Napier in great excitement. 'And now we know where the letter is hidden!'

'Do we?'

'Of course we do, man "Friend" can only mean his woman in Spain — he must have hidden the letter in her house. Pray God it has not been found! We must go to Gaucín at once; maybe we can find it-'

'I believe that the solution to the mystery lies here,' I said calmly, wandering around the room and examining the painting on the walls, which were mostly of hunting scenes and of horses. Napier shook his head at me in despair, and I continued: 'Think, Captain Napier, would you describe the woman you love as a "friend"?'

'No, I suppose not,' he said reluctantly, 'But who then could he possibly have meant? The Duke has made no other close attachments here. I was perhaps his closest confidant and he certainly did not give me the letter to hide!'

I did not answer, but asked instead: 'Has this room been kept locked since the Duke's disappearance?'

'As soon as we returned from the Hunt, we searched the room thoroughly, and it has been locked and guarded since,' said Napier impatiently, 'But surely we should be in Spain searching for the Duke!'

'We must be patient. Your men have been searching in Spain for over a week to no avail. We must seek clues here to the Duke's whereabouts. Now, you must arrange to leave the door of the room open, and withdraw the guard; then we will retire to the room across the corridor and await events.'

That evening we sat in that darkened room, with the door ajar, for several hours. Many of the servants of the Convent passed up and down the corridor, but none of them gave the Duke's room, with its open door, more than a passing glance. The maidservant Conchita passed, and stared curiously into the room; I felt Napier stir at my side, and put out a hand to restrain him as she passed on down the corridor. Then for a long while the corridor was empty.

Darkness was falling when a silent figure came furtively along the corridor towards the Duke's room. He stopped, looked from side to side, and then took down a painting from the wall outside the door and carried it into the room.

'Why, it is Barker, Father's batman!' whispered Napier in amazement. We crept across the hallway and in the gloom of the room opposite we could see the dim figure of the old soldier as he began to slit the back of the painting with a knife.

Before he could go any further we were upon him. When he saw us, he made no attempt to defend himself, but dropped the knife and fell on his knees to the floor, burying his head in his hands and crying over and over again:

'Forgive me, oh, forgive me. I was tempted, and I fell.'

In response to a call from Napier, servants came and took the weeping man away. I picked up the painting and showed it to my companion. It was the portrait of a noble chestnut stallion, and bore the name of the horse: "Caesar's Friend". I slipped my hand into the slit made by Barker's knife and gently pulled out a parchment and read its opening words to Robert Napier and his father, who had joined us:

'His Majesty King George, King of England and Elector of Hanover, to his most Catholic Majesty King Philip...'

'Mr. Holmes, I congratulate you,' said Lord Napier handsomely, 'But how will this help us to find the Duke?'

'Barker is the link, my Lord,' I replied. 'We must question him.'

The interrogation of the unfortunate Barker revealed what I had surmised. He had become addicted to gambling and had lost sums which were beyond his power to pay. His main creditor was a man called Ricoletti, who had indicated to Barker that he would accept payment in the form of little items of information about the Governor and his entourage.

'How could you do this, Barker!' said Lord Napier fiercely. 'You were once worthy of my trust!'

The old soldier cringed away from his master. 'Forgive me, my Lord,' he groaned, 'It seemed to be the only means I had of repaying my debts, and at first he was satisfied with trivial gossip, but then he began to demand more, and when I heard the Duke reading the letter I knew that this was the sort of information that Ricoletti wanted — the sort that he could sell to the Spaniards, and I went to him that very evening. How could I know that the devil would dare to kidnap the Duke -?"

'Enough, Barker,' interrupted Lord Napier sternly. 'You returned to steal the document, did you not? You are still in the pay of the Queen's enemies! Do not pretend remorse now."

'He promised that it was the last favour which I would have to do to pay off my debt, and that then I would be free,' said the old soldier desperately. 'I told him that I would not do it, and he replied with a laugh that if I did not find the letter the Duke would die and my part in the matter would be revealed. When we had searched the room I found a half-burnt scrap of paper in the fireplace. I concealed it and examined it later, but all I could read were the words "-sar's friend". I racked my brains over it, but I could make nothing of it, until tonight I remembered the painting outside the Duke's room -'

'You can help us now, and perhaps mitigate your punishment to some extent,' I said. 'Where can we find Ricoletti?'

'I do not know, sir,' said Barker earnestly, 'I believe he is a

Gibraltarian, but he lives in Spain, I don't know where, but I do know that he comes to Gibraltar after dark to visit taverns in the hope of picking up scraps of information which he can sell or use for blackmail. But I haven't seen him since the day he threatened me and demanded that I bring him the letter.'

'He must have taken fright at the hue and cry after the Duke's disappearance, and gone into hiding,' Lord Napier said wearily. 'We have no way of finding him. Take this man away.'

'If Ricoletti originally came from Gibraltar,' said I thoughtfully, as Barker was led away, 'Then he must be known to some Gibraltarians. I should like to question the maid Conchita and the Duke's groom.They may have some light to shed on this dark affair.'

The groom Pepe Ansaldo and the serving maid stood nervously some distance from each other, but the frequent glances they exchanged showed that there was a bond between them. Conspiracy or affection? I wondered. I questioned the groom, a dark-haired, handsome fellow, first, and heard how he had left the Duke as usual near the house of Ana Pedroz. When he had returned as arranged the house was deserted and no trace of the Duke or the woman could be found.

'Do you have any idea where your master may be?' I asked him.

His looked at me straight in the face and answered firmly, 'No, sir; if I had, I would have said so already. The Duke was good to me, and I would do anything to see him and the lady safe.'

Conchita looked admiringly at him for his bold words, and he flushed slightly and smiled at her reassuringly.

'You must realise,' I said, turning to her, 'That as one of the persons who heard about the letter, you are suspected of having given away the secret to the Duke's abductors.'

Conchita's clear brown eyes looked steadfastly at me, but she made no answer: she had no need to. Ansaldo came swiftly to her side, and taking her hand, said belligerently to me: 'Mr. Holmes, my Conchita had no part in this matter. and neither did I. We are true Gibraltarians; we are British, and we have no love for Spain!'

'I say, there, Ansaldo!' began Napier, shocked at the groom's boldness, but I motioned him to silence and said to the couple:

'I believe that you are both telling me the truth, and I know now that I can rely on your help to find the Duke; tell me now, do you know of a man called Ricoletti?'

The reaction from both of them showed that they did. 'He is a bad man, sir,' burst forth the maid, and Pepe nodded, adding, 'He was born with a club foot, and this seems to have embittered him, as if he blames the world around him for his infirmity. He was notorious in Gibraltar as a thief and a scoundrel and had to leave before justice caught up with him. He swore then that he would revenge himself on us, the Gibraltarians, for our treatment of him -'

'He's married to a Spanish woman, and she's worse than he is!' Conchita interrupted passionately. 'She used to look after babies here in Gibraltar, and several of them died mysteriously. People said that she dosed them with laudanum to keep them quiet, and gave them so much that they died of it! Nothing could be proved, but she and her husband had to leave Gibraltar after that.'

'A charming couple!' I remarked. 'Do you know where I can find them, for I am sure that where they are, there the Duke will be too!'

'They bought a derelict house in Gaucín,' said Pepe. 'They tried to make it into an inn, perhaps hoping to attract customers away from my cousin Pedro Real, whose hostelry is famous throughout Andalucía, but few travellers had the stomach to stay there more than once. The woman is a slattern, the inn was filthy and the food uneatable. and any customers who braved the bedbugs and the poisonous wine were soon driven away by the surly manners of the Ricolettis. They still live there, I believe, but it's no longer an inn.'

'But presumably it is large enough to conceal two prisoners!' I said. Ansaldo nodded, and I continued: 'I must go to Gaucln at once!'

'I will go with you! We'll take a well-armed band of officers -' said Robert Napier, but I shook my head firmly.

'The last thing we want is a hue and cry which will warn our quarry to flee, perhaps after murdering their prisoners.'

'Indeed not, and even were you successful, the news that an armed band of English soldiers had attacked a Spanish village would cause an international scandal which we certainly cannot afford,' stated Lord Napier firmly. 'But even if you are right and the Duke is in the power of this evil man, what can we do to free him, Mr. Holmes?'

'These people will not have any accomplices in this affair. They will want to keep their actions secret and also to avoid sharing out any reward they might hope to get. I think that two Spanish peasants arriving quietly in Gaucín at night could seek a night's lodging *chez* Ricoletti and soon find the captives and free them. I will need a companion who can speak fluent Spanish -"

'I will go with you, Mr. Holmes,' Pepe burst out. 'I know Gaucín and its people well, and I will do anything to help save the Duke from these fiends.'

A few hours later Pepe and I were riding along the rough track which led up the mountains towards Gaucín. Although it was November, the weather was warm and dry. We passed by groves of olive trees, and then the track led upwards into the mountains and was lined and in some places almost roofed over by cork oaks and carob trees, the latter heavy with dark brown pods. These soon gave way to pines, and the breeze in our faces took on a chilly bite.

'There's Gaucín!' called Pepe, who was riding just ahead.

I spurred my patient steed until I caught up with him at the top of the rise. The white houses of Gaucín were strung along the next ridge ahead of us, ending with the stark ruined walls of the castle, which was built on the very edge of a sheer rocky precipice that overlooked the valley below. On the horizon in the far distance the faint outline of the Rock of Gibraltar could be seen.

A few minutes later we were riding up the main and indeed the only street in Gaucín and shortly afterwards we were comfortably ensconced in the parlour of the 'Hostal Inglés' where we were royally entertained by Pepe's cousin, Pedro Real, who was a colourful character with bristling moustachios and a tremendous paunch, and who kept pressing us repeatedly to drink the raw local brandy. Eventually I was able to get him on to the subject of Ricoletti.

'Ah, that scoundrel,' he said scornfully, spitting into the roaring log fire in front of us, 'He thought he could take my livelihood from me, with that miserable excuse for an inn that he opened! He failed, of course, but he still sits there dreaming of making his fortune and hatching plots with that harridan of a wife of his.'

'Are they there now?' I asked quickly, as he paused for breath.

'They must be. I heard him coming up the road late one night, with two heavily laden donkeys — why, it must have been the night the Duke disappeared! Do you think -?'

'It seems very likely that the Duke and Senora Pedroz were rendered insensible by this evil couple and are now held somewhere in their house.'

'But that cannot be!' Pepe burst out, 'I went there with the *guardia* on the next morning and watched while he searched the place. Not even a mouse could have escaped his eye! The Ricolettis were not there and no captives were hidden there.'

'They must be there,' protested Pedro Real, 'I would surely have heard them if they had passed this way, and there is no other way out of Gaucín than the street which passes this house.

'Perhaps a hidden cellar -' I suggested.

'Impossible!' stated Pedro Real with finality. 'I remember when that house was built. It sits firmly on the solid rock of the crag, just below the castle. There is no cellar underneath it. You would need gunpowder to blast a hole in that rock and the village would surely have noticed if that fool Ricoletti had tried!' he added with a laugh.

'Well. we must go and see this place,' I said.

'I will come with you,' said Pedro Real, wheezing slightly as he heaved himself out of his chair.

A few minutes later, the three of us crept up the unpaved street leading towards the Ricolettis' house. It was pitch dark by now and only a few faint flickering lights from the windows of the houses we passed served to illuminate our way. But no light shone from the Ricoletti's house when we arrived there. It lay there, squat and black, with the greater blackness of the ruined castle looming over it. Pedro

Real stood well back as Pepe and I approached in our guise of travelling peasants and knocked at the door. We knocked and knocked again, but there was no answer, and nothing stirred within.

Pepe and I put our shoulders to the door, but it would not budge. Then Pedro lumbered up and added his considerable weight to our efforts. The wood around the lock splintered and we were inside. Lighting lamps which we had brought with us, we looked around. The house was in disorder but it was the disorder of slatternly neglect rather than signs of a struggle. The only movement was of the cockroaches on the table, attracted by the mouldering remains of food which lay there. There was a general smell of decay but over it all a faint sweetish odour reached my nostrils. It came from a corner of the room we were in, where a dirty cloth lay, with a small bottle by its side.

Lifting these to my nose, I sniffed cautiously, and then exclaimed: 'Chloroform! That's how they overcame the Duke and the lady. Now we know that they were here; but where can they be now?'

'Perhaps they have been spirited away from Gaucín,' Pepe suggested gloomily, 'They may be miles away by now.'

'Never!' Pedro Real insisted. 'I've told you, I heard them go up the street that night, but I didn't hear them return, and I miss nothing that passes my house by night or day. They must be here somewhere; there is no other way out of Gaucín.'

'If they did not go down the street, they must have gone up it,' I remarked, 'What lies beyond this house?'

'Only the castle,' said Pedro Real, 'But it is ruined and uninhabited. No one could live there.'

'Nevertheless, since we have eliminated all other possibilities, the castle it must be,' I told them. 'We will go there now.'

We left the house and continued up the street carrying our lanterns and were soon clambering over the loose stones which had fallen away from the crumbling ramparts of the castle. The autumn breeze had stiffened into an icy wind, and rain began to fall. No light was visible within the castle as we passed silently through the gate, and Pepe muttered 'Surely they can't be in here!'

I held up my hand for silence and listened. At first I could hear nothing except for the whispering of the wind in the trees and an occasional bark from a restless dog in the village below us. Then I became conscious of the murmuring of voices, which seemed to come from beneath our feet. I threw myself to the ground and pressed my ear to the cold flags, while my two companions gaped, evidently thinking that I had taken leave of my senses, but I was able to satisfy myself that the voices were coming from directly beneath our feet.

'What lies below here?' I asked Pedro.

'Why, nothing,' he answered in surprise, but then almost immediately added, 'Wait! I remember now; there are some steps leading downwards just beyond this arch in front of us, but for as long as I can remember they have been blocked by stones which must have fallen from the walls many years ago.'

We hurried through the arch and looked around. There, to the side, was a flight of stairs apparently leading into the bowels of the earth. We stepped over a pile of stones and I cautiously shone my lantern down the stairwell to illuminate our descent. The stairs appeared to have been cleared recently; no doubt this explained the pile of stones at the stairhead. I signalled to my companions and we began to creep down silently. At the foot of the stairs was a wooden door which looked new; Ricoletti had evidently cleared away the rubble secretly and put in this door so that he could use this secret place for his evil purposes. I pushed gently against the door, which swung silently inwards, and drawing a pistol from my belt I stepped into the room.

For a few seconds none of the occupants was aware of my intrusion, and I was able to look around. The room was barely and meanly furnished with two straw pallets and two chairs. On each of these a prisoner was bound — a pale and defiant young man, who in spite of the bruises and dried blood which covered his face and head was easily recognisable as the Duke, and on the second chair a young black-haired woman lay limply with her eyes closed. A knife was held to her neck by an evil-looking squint-eyed woman who laughed as the point pierced the skin, and a red trickle of blood ran down and began to drip on to the floor. Standing menacingly over the Duke was a villainous looking, heavily built man with a club foot who was saying:

'Very well, my little princeling, if we cannot get your secret by starving you or by beating you, perhaps we can find another way to make you sing: Tell me where you have hidden the letter, or my dear wife will cut the lady's throat!'

The Duke struggled vainly with his bonds, and cried out hoarsely 'No!', but whether this was a further refusal to co-operate, or an appeal to save his Ana, we never found out, for at that moment Ricoletti turned and saw me standing at the door. Growling angrily, he came at me with a lumbering, clumsy rush, but I clapped the muzzle of my pistol to his forehead, and he stopped and stood stock still, trembling with fear and rage.

The woman turned, her face distorted with hate, and screeched in broken English: 'Let him go, or I keel the girl!'

I turned to her, and said, more coolly than I actually felt: 'Madam, if another drop of the lady's blood falls to the floor. I will blow your husband's brains out. Drop the knife!'

Behind that mask of evil some sort of love for her unsavoury spouse must have been hidden, for with a curse she let the knife fall to the ground, and I let out my breath in a sigh of relief. But the exchange had distracted my attention from Ricoletti, who flung me to the ground and leapt for the door. He did not get far, however, for at the foot of the steps he cannoned into Pedro Real's enormous paunch, which almost filled the stairway, and fell back into the room. Pepe Ansaldo stepped forward and struck him sharply on the head with the butt of his pistol and he fell to the ground unconscious, while I recovered my own weapon before Mrs. Ricoletti could reach it. Pepe covered the evil couple with his gun while I freed the Duke and Sra. Pedroz, who was already recovering from her faint.

Later, after our prisoners had been delivered to the *guardia* of Gaucín, my companions and I sat with the Duke in the parlour of the 'Hostal Inglés', while Pedro's wife tended to Ana Pedroz, who was weak from hunger and ill-treatment, for the Ricolettis had tried to starve their prisoners into submission, before they had tortured the Duke in a vain attempt to force him to tell where he had hidden the letter.

'The letter! We must make sure that it has not been found by one of Ricoletti's minions,' said the Duke anxiously, and I hastened to reassure him.

'Do not fear, your Royal Highness, it is in Lord Napier's safe in Gibraltar where I placed it after I had discovered it in the place where you had hidden it.'

'Mr. Holmes, you are a marvel!' said the Duke. 'I'm sure I left no clue to guide you. How did you find the letter?'

'I have my methods, Sir,' I replied.

* * *

"That was an amazing tale, Holmes!" I remarked when he had finished, "And the most surprising aspect of it is that no whisper of this affair has ever reached the newspapers, either in Spain or in England. Quite apart from the scandal which would have been caused to our Royal family if the Duke's illicit affair had come to light, think of the political implications of that letter -"

"More than one person in Gibraltar must have known of the story," said Sherlock Holmes quietly, "But the people of Gibraltar are above all loyal subjects of the British Crown. They would not dream of embarrassing our Queen by making the matter public, and even less would they consider doing anything which might weaken the links between England and the Rock to which they are so passionately attached."

"I am still curious about one thing," I said pensively, "You did not say what became of Señora Pedroz."

"Ah, Watson, you were always an incurable romantic, and I did not want to disappoint you," said my friend with a laugh. "Ana Pedroz had already told the Duke before they were abducted that she intended to marry an elderly banker from the town of Ronda, who knew of her liaison with the Duke but was prepared to forgive it because of his love for her. She was a practical lady, and realised that there was no future in continuing an affair with a Duke who would never be allowed to marry her, although he did love her, I believe. We took the Duke back with us to Gibraltar, and from there he travelled directly to England, carrying the letter with him. I sometimes wonder what he told his Royal mother about the whole affair. As far as I am aware he never set eyes on the lady again."

ALSO PUBLISHED BY GIBRALTAR BOOKS

THE BIRDS OF GIBRALTAR
   by J. E. Cortés, J. C. Finlayson, M. A. Mosquera, E. F. J. Garcia
A valuable study of the bird life and migration patterns in this ornithologically
strategic area.   £4.95

THE GUNS AND TOWERS OF GIBRALTAR
   by George Palao
A study of the development of the Moorish Castle and other features of the
fortifications of Gibraltar, and the ordnance employed on its batteries during
the last three centuries.   £2.95

THE ROCK OF THE GIBRALTARIANS: A HISTORY OF GIBRALTAR
   by General Sir William G. F. Jackson
The most up-to-date history of Gibraltar by a leading military historian, with
16 maps, 30 drawings and 39 photographs.   £11.95

CENTREPORT GIBRALTAR
   by A. A. & D. M. Sloma assisted by S. Johnson
A guide to sailing in the Strait with plans of the harbours in the area and along
the west coast of Morocco. With folding charts of the Strait and the Moroccan
coast.   £16.95

THE FORTRESS CAME FIRST
   by Thomas Finlayson
A study by the Government Archivist of the evacuation of the civilian
population of Gibraltar during the last war.   £14.95

GIBGUIDES
Handy guides to Gibraltar, lavishly illustrated with coloured photographs.
No. 1 GIBRALTAR GUIDEBOOK by T. Benady   £2.50
No.2 THE FLOWERS AND WILDLIFE OF GIBRALTAR
   by J. Cortés and C. Finlayson   £2.95
No.3 GUIDE TO THE GIBRALTAR MUSEUM by T. Benady   £1.95

THE WESTERN SEPHARDIM: the second volume of THE SEPHARDI
HERITAGE
   Edited by Richard Barnett and Walter Schwab
The history of a number of Jewish communities formed by exiles from Spain.
                                                                       £35.00